One Day I Went Rambling

Kelly Bennett

illustrations by

Terri Murphy

bright sky press
HOUSTON, TEXAS

2365 Rice Boulevard, Suite 202,
Houston, Texas 77005

ISBN 978-1-936474-06-6

10 9 8 7 6 5 4 3 2 1

Library of Congress Cataloging-in-Publication Data on file with publisher
Editorial Direction, Lucy Herring Chambers
Creative Direction, Ellen Peeples Cregan
Illustrations, Terri Murphy
Printed in China by RR Donnelley

For my niece Grace,
with her huge imagination and heart to match!

With a nod to Valine Hobbs
whose poetry inspired me to write this story

- *Kelly Bennett*

For my father and his love of broken, cast-off things,
who first showed me how to ramble

- *Terri Murphy*

One day I went rambling
and found a shining star.

Saucer's Crest...

“A hubcap,” said Lamar.

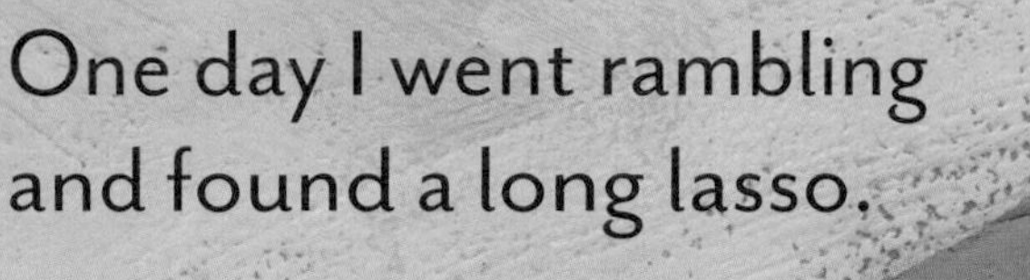

One day I went rambling
and found a long lasso.

A cowpoke's twirling rope:

"A strand of vine," said Beau.

"You're crazy!" my friends told me,
making fun of all my finds.
They said, "Why go rambling?"
"It's just a waste of time."

Still, I kept rambling
and found a shining band.

"An old pop top," said Tran.

Huck

One day I went rambling
and found a wooden barge.

Finn's trusty craft

"A packing crate," said Marj.

One day I went rambling
and found a bright white sheet.

"That's Granny's slip," said Pete.

"What's up, Zane?" my friends asked me.

"Whatcha doing with all that stuff?"

I smile and said, “It’s secret.”
“You’ll find out soon enough.”

Next time I went rambling,
so did Scott and Jess and Beau.
They peeked around the corner.
I pretended not to know.

I went right on rambling
and found a smooth, brown vest.

"A mighty warrior's shield."

"Hey that's cool!" called Jess.

Next time we went rambling
along came Marj and Tran.
We found some flutter plumes.

A Spanish Dancer's fan.

“Look here,” Lamar called out,
holding up a rusty pot.
“Is this one of your treasures?”
“Ignore him,” whispered Scott.

MONKEY

We kept right on rambling
and found a long, white tooth.
“A broken comb,” said Lu.

said Ruth.

One day we went rambling
and found some sparkling stone.
"Wow, what are these?" asked Pete.

"Priceless jewels,"

said Joan.

Next time we went rambling
we took our treasures, too.
“Gather round,” I told my friends.
“There’s lots of work to do.”

"Wait up!" Lamar and Lu called out.
"We won't poke fun at you.
We're ready for adventure.
Can we come rambling too?"

"Ahoy Mates, time's a-wasting.

Climb aboard! Let's sail away.
We'll explore the world together,
finding adventure along the way."

"Hey! What's that?"